Weekly Reader Children's Book Club presents

Pirates in the Park

BY
Thom Roberts

Pictures by Harold Berson

CROWN PUBLISHERS, INC., NEW YORK

For
Wyatt and Lawrence
T.R.

It was warm and sunny the day Jenny said to her dog Mose, "Let's go to the park." Mose watched and wagged his tail while Jenny piled her stuffed animals and dolls inside the wagon. "You all need a little exercise. Especially you," she said to two tin soldiers as she polished them on her shirttail. Just then a very fat elephant fell from the top of the pile. Jenny picked it up by its trunk. "And you really need some exercise."

Mose followed the wagon as Jenny pulled it to the park.
When they got to the boat pond, Jenny saw a group of kids. They
were watching a boy launch his new pirate ship. "The *Skull* can
outsail and outshoot any vessel on the seven seas," he boasted.
"Shiver me timbers, mates—you can watch, but don't touch her."

Jenny pulled the wagon close to the pond. A gust of wind
filled the sails of the pirate ship and it cut through the ripples
toward an island in the middle of the pond. "I wish I had a boat,"
she said, "even a little one."

Mose wagged his tail and sniffed the ground. Jenny took the elephant from the wagon. "Wouldn't you like a ship like that?" she said, putting the elephant on the grass. After she had put the other animals and dolls near the edge of the pond, Mose nudged her and ran ahead a few feet. "I'll play with you in a minute," she said. Mose ran back toward her and dropped a walnut shell at her feet.

She turned the shell over in her hands—then she smiled. Mose looked on quietly as she picked up a twig and a maple leaf. She poked the twig through the leaf and stuck it into a piece of walnut meat that was left in the shell. "We can call it the S.S. *Walnut*," said Jenny.

She leaned over the pond and put the little ship on the water.
It didn't sink...but it didn't cut through the ripples the way
the *Skull* did either.

The boy who had just launched the *Skull* watched her for a few
moments and laughed. "You call that a ship!" he shouted.
The others began to laugh too.

Jenny tried and tried to push the S.S. *Walnut* out on the pond, but the lapping water kept holding it back.

"You need a real ship—like mine!" yelled the boy.

"Yeah," shouted another boy, "go home and play with your dolls!" He threw a stone at the S.S. *Walnut*.

Jenny's face got redder and redder as she leaned closer to the S.S. *Walnut* and gave it another push. Then, suddenly, she noticed the reflection of her ship in the water.

Somehow it looked different. It seemed bigger.
And it *was* bigger—right before her eyes it grew and grew
until it was full sized.

Waves were now slapping against the ship. Jenny turned and saw all her animals and dolls marching on board. She was the captain and they were her crew. Mose followed behind her as she walked up the gangplank.

While the crew made ready to set sail, Jenny and Mose stood at the ship's helm and sighted their course. A rag doll pulled the gangplank aboard. The elephant lifted the anchor. Then slowly the huge ship pulled away from the dock.

The S.S. *Walnut*'s sails were full in the breeze as it headed out to sea. Jenny stood proud at the helm and guided the ship toward an island on the horizon.

The crew was working peacefully when suddenly a rabbit ran toward Jenny and handed her a telescope. "Look! Out there!" he shouted.

Jenny focused the telescope and there,
hiding in a cove of the island, was the *Skull*.

The S.S. *Walnut*'s crew was terrified.

A giraffe hid its face in a sail,

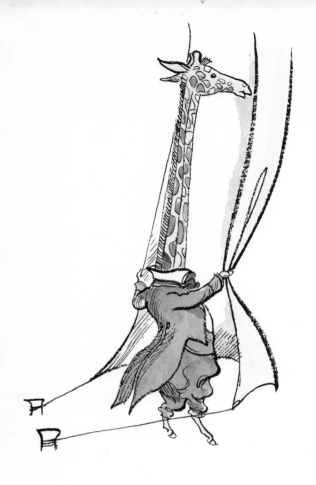

the two tin soldiers deserted their posts,

and a clown ran around in circles.

Even Mose looked scared.

But Jenny stayed at the helm.
"Full speed ahead!" she commanded.
"And back to your stations, all of you!"

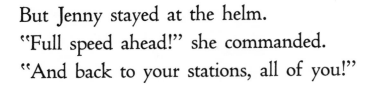

As they neared the island, the *Skull* sailed
out from its hiding place in the cove. Jenny
looked through the telescope and recognized the boy
from the pond in the park. He held his sword up,
and the pirates aimed their cannons at
the S.S. *Walnut*.

No one on the S.S. *Walnut* knew what to do. Then the pirate captain slashed his sword through the air and the cannons began firing.

Over and over the cannons boomed as the *Skull* sailed
closer to the S.S. *Walnut*. Huge cannonballs
splashed in the water, then one hit the mainsail
of the S.S. *Walnut*.

"Surrender!" shrieked the elephant.
"We don't have a chance!"

A pig was running around in circles.

The clown was turning somersaults

and the rag doll shouted, "We'll all have to walk the plank!" Even Jenny looked worried.

The *Skull* kept gaining on them and soon it was alongside the S.S. *Walnut*. Just when Jenny thought they would have to surrender, Mose crouched with his front feet on the gunwale. Then he suddenly leaped toward the other ship and knocked the pirate captain to the deck.

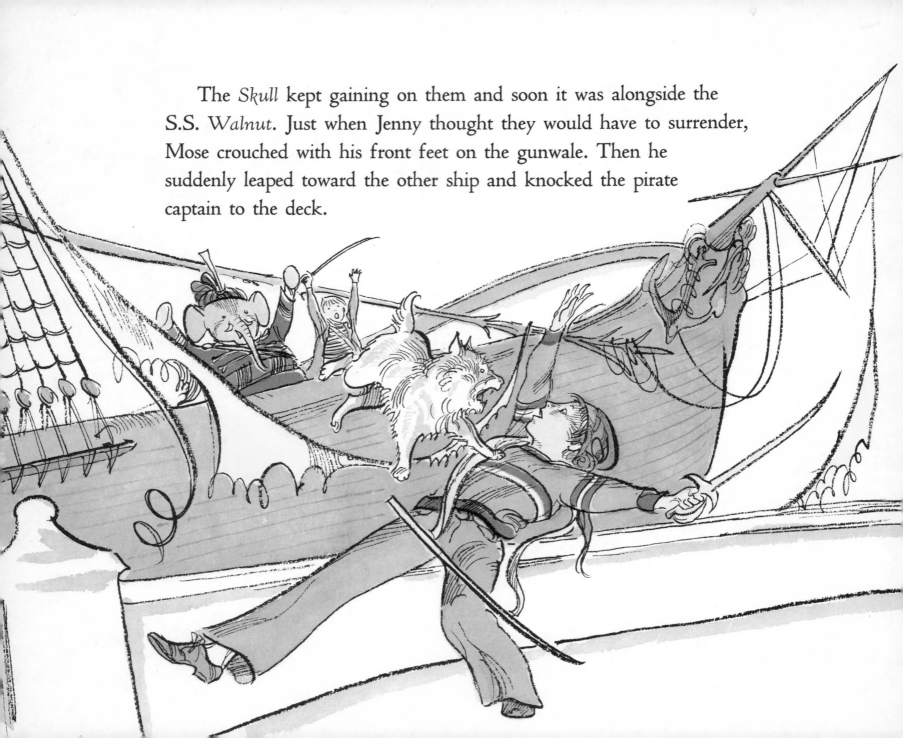

The other pirates tripped over one another as they
ran to help their captain.

"Now's our chance! Straighten up and full speed ahead!"
yelled Jenny as the S.S. *Walnut* began to pull away from the *Skull*.
"Hurry, Mose! Jump aboard." But it was too late. The pirates
had pulled Mose from their captain and were
holding him captive.

The S.S. *Walnut* pulled farther and farther away from the *Skull*
and Jenny steered it toward a river that flowed through the island.
But the *Skull* started after them again. Jenny knew her ship
should try to outrun it, but she couldn't leave Mose behind.

"Drop anchor," Jenny shouted, just when the S.S. *Walnut* was about to get away from the pirates.

At this, a ballerina who had been dancing around and around began to cry.

The rabbit covered his eyes with his paws and leaped down the hatch.

A bear played dead.

And everyone else cried, "Don't stop!"

"Back to your stations," Jenny shouted firmly. "And aim those cannons at that big tree."

The crew obeyed, and when the *Skull* was under the tree,
Jenny yelled, "Fire!"

Their aim was perfect. The giant tree swayed for a moment, then slowly began falling toward the *Skull*. It tore through the masts and sails, then boards creaked and split as the tree crushed the deck. "Jump!" cried the pirate captain.

Mose jumped overboard with the pirates and swam toward the S.S. *Walnut* where the crew was waiting to help him aboard.

A giraffe stretched its neck over the gunwale and lowered its head to the water. Mose clung to the giraffe's long neck with his front legs and was lifted aboard.

"Hurrah!" shouted the crew as the *Skull* began to sink. The elephant picked Jenny and Mose up with his trunk and put them on his back.

The bear and the ballerina danced around the deck.
The tin soldiers saluted Mose and Jenny while
everyone else cheered and laughed.

When Jenny saw that the pirates had made
it safely to shore, she said it was time to sail
for home. The crew manned their posts and
the S.S. *Walnut* sailed past the crushed
Skull which was disappearing under the
river's surface. Then, when they were
well under way, Jenny said, "It's good
to be going home." She hugged Mose
and closed her eyes as he licked her face.

"Hey, that's a neat elephant," said a little boy.

"Will you show us how to make a boat like that?" asked a girl.

Jenny opened her eyes and saw she was holding the tiny
S.S. *Walnut* in the palm of her hand.

Several grown-ups and older kids were staring at the boy who had
waded into the pond to get his pirate ship. It had been
crushed by a floating log.

The other kids gathered around Jenny and began playing with
Mose, Jenny's toys, and, of course, with the S.S. *Walnut*.